This is the Wind

Liz Rosenberg   Illustrated by Renée Reichert

A NEAL PORTER BOOK
ROARING BROOK PRESS
NEW YORK

This is the wind that blew on the farm

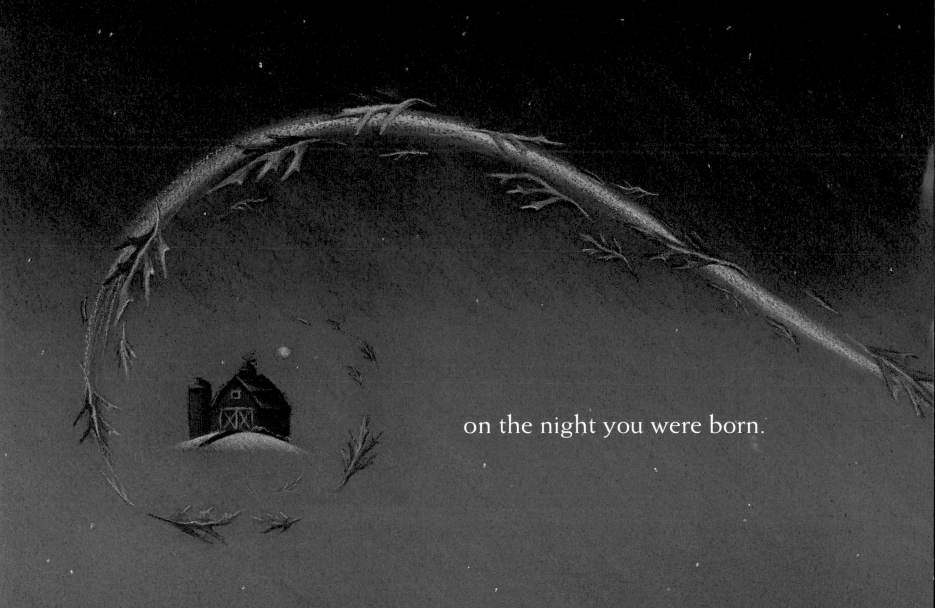

on the night you were born.

This is the mouse that
crawled in the house

to stay nice and warm

from the wind that blew on the farm on the night you were born.

This is the man who walked all around

to follow the sound

of a little mouse who crawled in the house

to stay nice and warm

from the wind that blew on the farm

on the night you were born.

This is the wife who startled awake

and wanted some cake

with the man who walked all around

to follow the sound

of a little mouse who crawled in the house to stay nice and warm

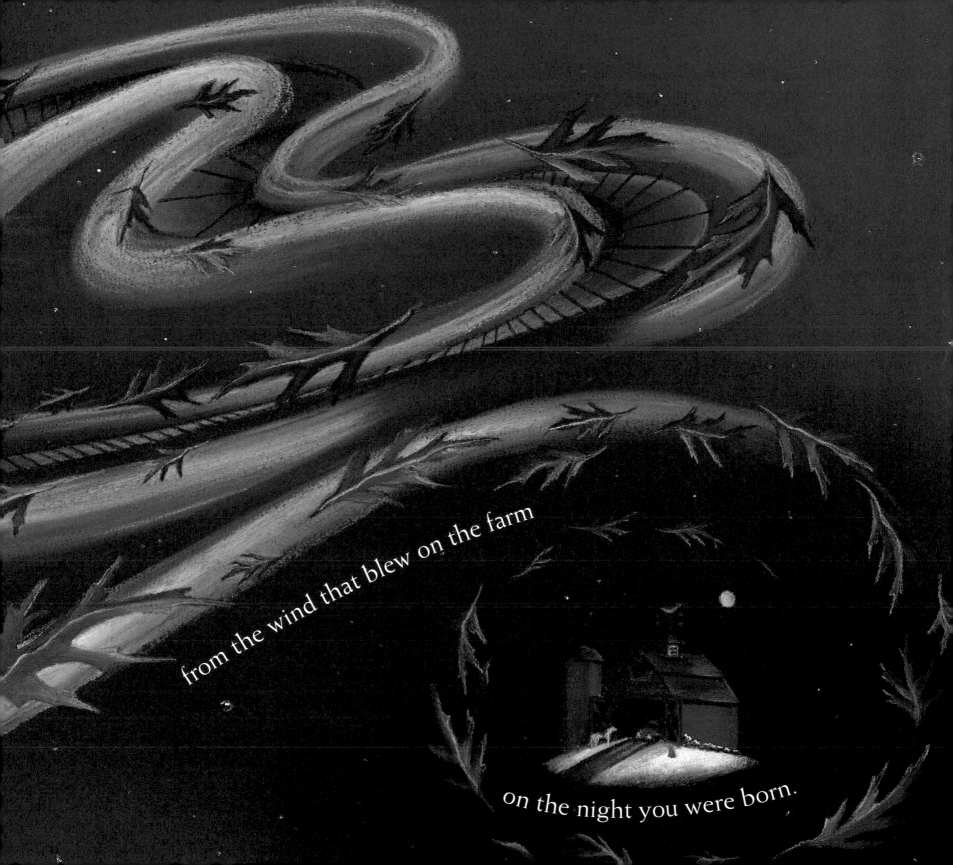

from the wind that blew on the farm

on the night you were born.

This is the road,
so icy and cold

that carried the wife who startled awake

and wanted some cake

with the man who walked all around

to follow the sound

of a little mouse who crawled in the house to stay nice and warm

from the wind that blew on the farm on the night you were born.

This is the place as white as new lace

at the end of the road, so icy and cold

that carried the wife who startled awake

and wanted some cake

with the man who walked all around to follow the sound

of a little mouse who crawled

in the house

to stay nice and warm

from the wind that blew on the farm on the night you were born.

This is your cry

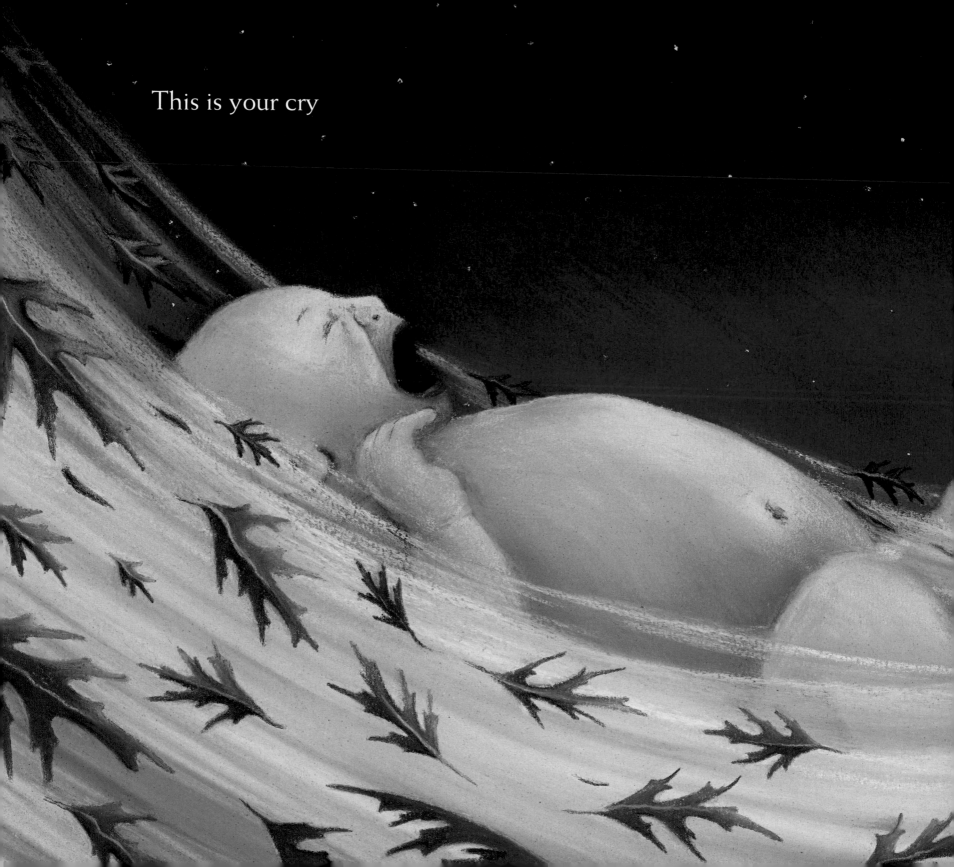

that rose to the sky

in that busy place as white as fine lace

at the end of the road, so icy and cold

that carried the wife who startled awake

and wanted some cake

with the man who walked all around to follow the sound

of a little mouse who crawled in the house

to stay nice and warm

from the wind

which grew calm

on the night you were born.

For Lily, for Lily, for Lily—L. R.
For Matthew and Sarah Rose—R. R.

Text copyright © 2008 by Liz Rosenberg

Illustrations copyright © 2008 by Renée Reichert

A Neal Porter Book

Published by Roaring Brook Press

Roaring Brook Press is a division of Holtzbrinck Publishing Holdings Limited Partnership

175 Fifth Avenue, New York, New York 10010

www.roaringbrookpress.com

Distributed in Canada by H. B. Fenn and Company, Ltd.

Cataloging-in-Publication Data is on file at the Library of Congress

ISBN-13: 978-1-59643-268-0

ISBN-10: 1-59643-268-3

Roaring Brook Press books are available for special promotions and premiums.

For details, contact: Director of Special Markets, Holtzbrinck Publishers.

Printed in China

First edition October 2008

2 4 6 8 10 9 7 5 3 1